AF601227
ENDANGERED
WEAPON B
VOLUME 1
MECHANIMAL SCIENCE
DAVID TALLERMAN
BOB MOLESWORTH

 Published by Markosia Enterprises, PO BOX 3477, Barnet, Hertfordshire, EN5 9HN. FIRST PRINTING, July 2013. Harry Markos, Director.

ISBN: 978-1-909276-08-6

ENDANGERED WEAPON B

Written by:
David Tallerman
Art by:
Bob Molesworth

For Markosia Enterprises Ltd

HARRY MARKOS
Publisher & Managing Partner

IAN SHARMAN
GM JORDAN
ANDY BRIGGS
Group Editors

INTRODUCTION
By
Paul Cornell

Endangered Weapon B is a deeply silly comic, in a world where there aren't enough deeply silly comics. Wryness is my favourite thing, and so I find great satisfaction here in everything from the alphabetical list of experimental subjects to the continual expression of angry concentration on the face of that bear. My favourite movies include The Pirates in an Adventure with Scientists and The Fifth Element, and that vein of sighing and exasperated engagement with an absurd world is something shared by EWB. I mean, look at that title, which does several things at once and includes so many tasty contradictions.

EWB also engages with the whole narrative of the British colonial man of science going out and protecting the empire through his discoveries... by pushing those tropes to their fullest extent and making them pop. Where Tilly got that raptor who knows, but the sight of it on the hockey field says everything. Unlike in the real world, she is absolutely unburdened by the demands of her 'master', and her being like that, and that feeling so odd, points an arrow at what the real world version of all this might be. Our 'hero' is so untroubled by ethics he's willing to live and let live with the Nazis.

At times, EWB feels like a game of Exquisite Corpse in comics form, David Tallerman just yelling 'and then... and then -!' with every page turn, as if daring himself to come up with something even more absurd, built only on the shoulders of what just happened. I heartily commend this sort of thing. And I hope it continues its deep silliness for a long time.

Paul Cornell,
Buckinghamshire, May 2013.

Paul Cornell is one the world's leading authorities on writing deep silliness, having penned such classically bonkers comic books as Captain Britain and MI:13 for Marvel and Knight and Squire for DC. He's also the acclaimed author of two original novels, episodes of Robin Hood, Primeval and Doctor Who (for which he received a Hugo nomination) and many other fine comics, including runs on Black Widow, Demon Knights and Wolverine.

Details of all that and more can be found at his website, www.paulcornell.com.

WHO WOULD HAVE GUESSED THAT THE HIDDEN WING OF THE LIBRARY OF ALEXANDRIA WOULD BE HERE IN THE WILDS OF AUSTRALIA?
TIK
ONLY YOU ... PROFESSOR.
TIK
I WAS THE ONE WHO BLOODY FOUND IT!

ENDANGERED WEAPON B
AND THE TENTACLES OF DOOM
STORY: DAVID TALLERMAN
ART: BOB MOLESWORTH

TAK
TAK
TINK
!!!
RUUMBLE
CHONK
RUMBLE
RUMBLE

SMASH!!!
ARISTOTLE ON VOODOO
WELL, THAT WAS UNEXPECTEDLY STRAIGHTFORWARD.
NOT SO FAST!

YOU SHALL NOT TOUCH THAT.
GO, SQUID SQUAD 7!

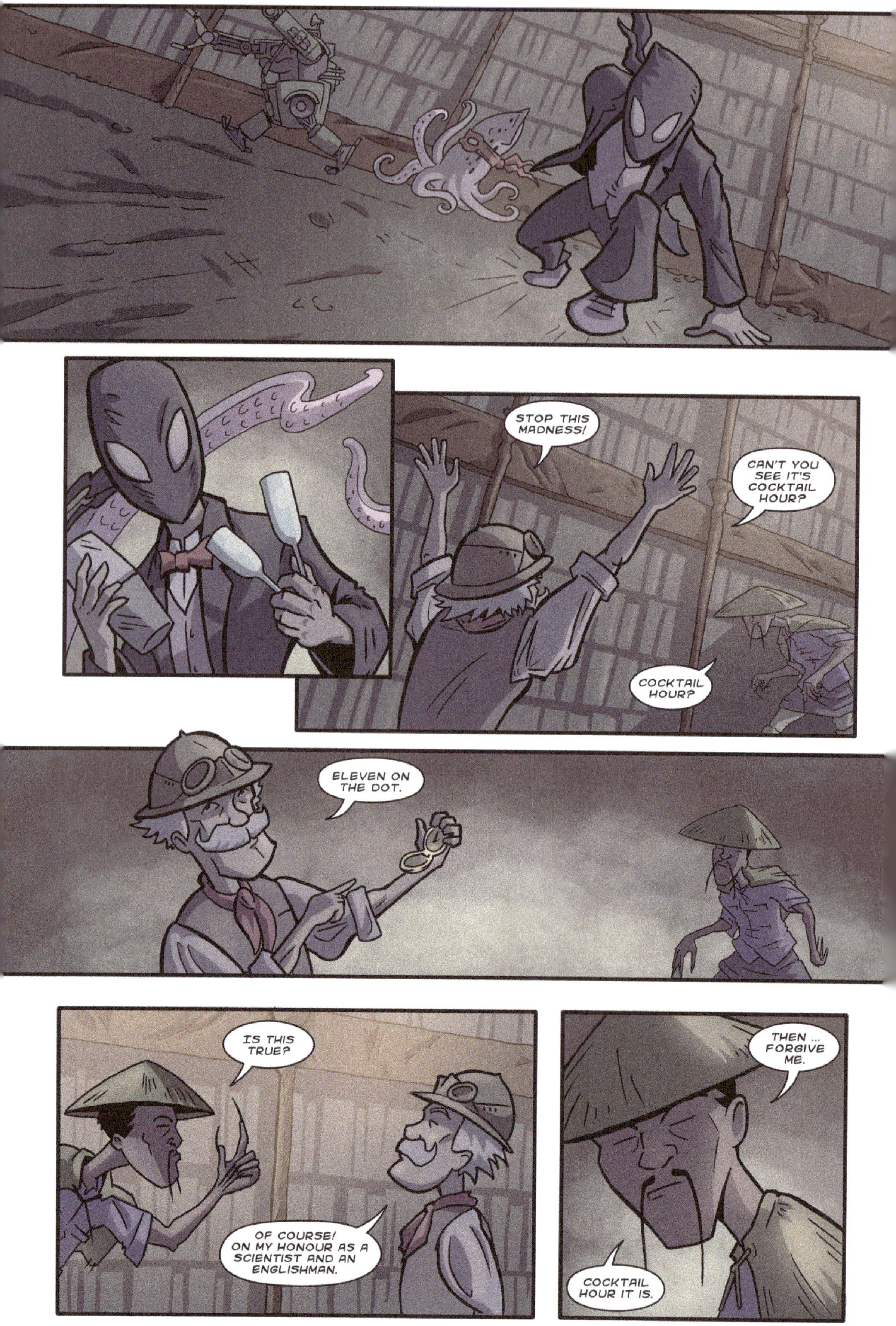

STOP THIS MADNESS!
CAN'T YOU SEE IT'S COCKTAIL HOUR?
COCKTAIL HOUR?
ELEVEN ON THE DOT.

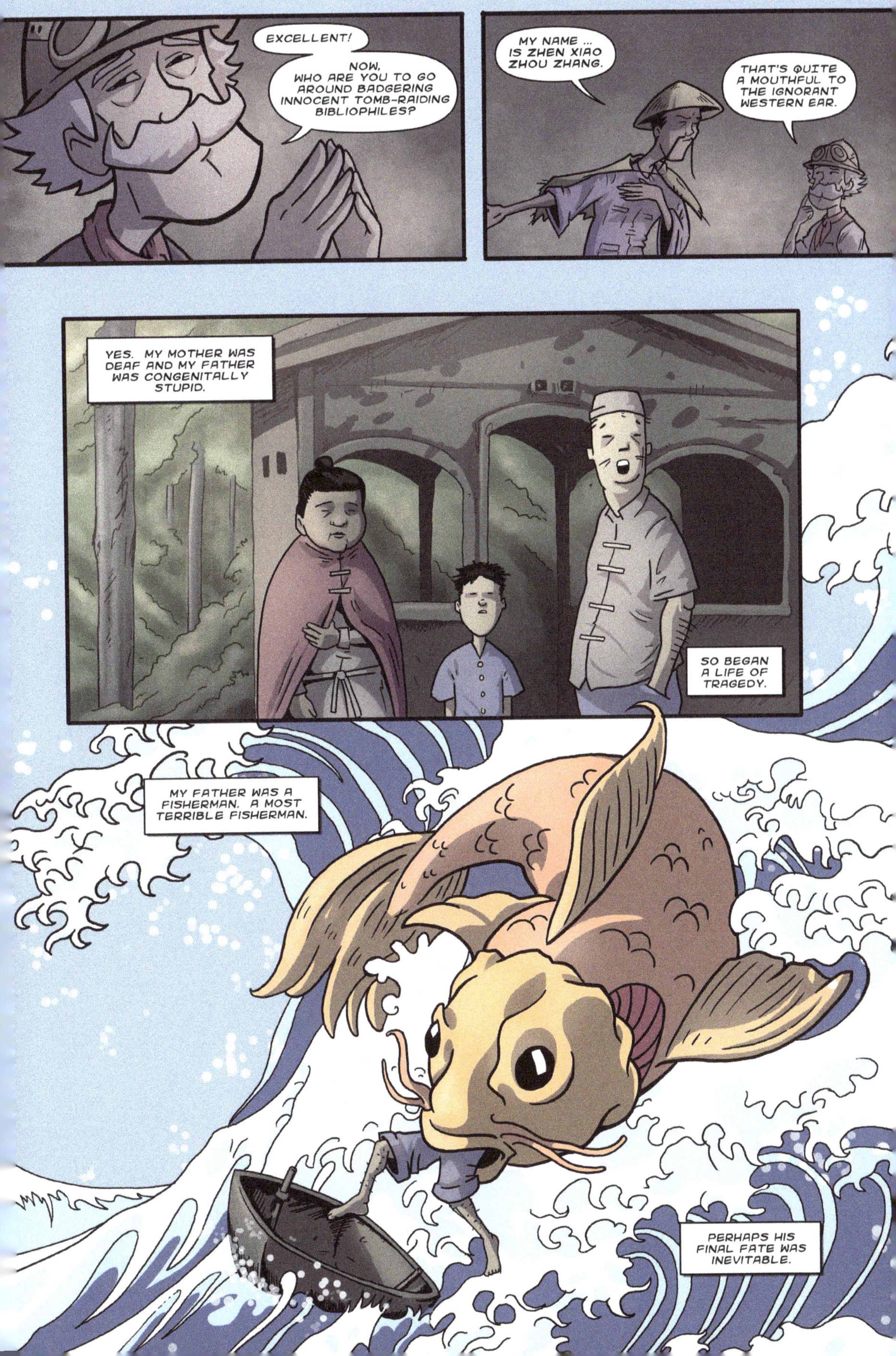

YES. MY MOTHER WAS DEAF AND MY FATHER WAS CONGENITALLY STUPID.

SO BEGAN A LIFE OF TRAGEDY.

MY FATHER WAS A FISHERMAN. A MOST TERRIBLE FISHERMAN.

PERHAPS HIS FINAL FATE WAS INEVITABLE.

SO IT FELL TO ME, HIS ONLY SON, TO INHERIT MY FATHER'S TRADE - AND HIS POVERTY.
TRY AS I MIGHT, I COULD NEVER CHANGE MY FORTUNE.
THE YEARS PASSED BY, EACH MORE POINTLESS AND PITILESS THAN THE LAST...
...UNTIL THE DAY CAME WHEN I COULD BEAR MY HARDSHIPS NO MORE.

AS WOEFULLY INTERESTING AS YOUR STORY IS, I DO BELIEVE THE COCKTAILS ARE READY.
WHAT IS THIS? WHAT DOES IT CONTAIN?

OH, ALCOHOL MOSTLY. A DASH OF LAUDANUM. I CALL IT AN ICE GIANT. BEST NOT TO EAT THE MINT, IT'S ONLY THERE FOR COLOUR.

KNOW THIS, PROFESSOR.
IT IS NO MERE COINCIDENCE I SHOULD BE WAITING HERE TO FOIL YOU. I KNEW YOU WOULD COME TO STEAL FROM THIS ANCIENT PLACE OF LEARNING.
AND WE ARE VOWED TO STOP YOU, MY CRIME-FIGHTING SQUID AND I.

WELL, EACH TO HIS OWN, EH?
I'M SURE ALL THAT NONSENSE CAN WAIT FOR LATER.
NOW, HOW'S YOUR ICE GIANT?

I BELIEVE I CAN TASTE MY TEETH.

EXCELLENT!

PROFESSOR, IF WE ARE AGREED UPON THIS PERIOD OF TRUCE, PERHAPS YOU WILL TELL ME HOW YOU MET YOUR MOST UNUSUAL COMPANIONS?
MIGHT I ASK HOW YOU CAME BY THIS LITHE AND DUSKY BEAUTY?
HEY! MUCKY OLD...
OH, THAT'S JUST TILLY. TILLY IS MY CHIEF ENGINEER AND PROSPECTIVE FUTURE WIFE.
NEVER GONNA HAPPEN!
HMM ... WELL, THERE'S A STORY THERE, I SUPPOSE.
I WAS IN THE POLYNESIAN ISLANDS, VISITING A RECENTLY DISCOVERED TRIBE TO EXTEND THE CIVILIZED HAND OF CHARITY.
<LO, PRIMITIVE ISLAND FOLK, I AM THE GREAT GOD FROM THE SKIES.>
<GIVE ME YOUR WORSHIP AND YOUR PRECIOUS SHINY DOODADS, AND I SHALL MAKE THE COCONUTS SWELL IN THE TREES AND THE FISH DANCE IN YOUR NETS!>
<NO GODS TODAY, THANK YOU.>
<WE'RE QUITE HAPPY WITH THE ONE WE HAVE.>
COCONUTS ... SWELL IN ... TREES!
FISH ... DANCE IN ... NETS!

<WHO COULD HAVE BUILT SUCH AN UNLIKELY MARVEL?>
<THAT'D BE ME.>
<IS THAT ... A SENTIENT COMPUTER? MADE ENTIRELY FROM VEGETABLE MATTER?>
<SURE IS!>

<REMARKABLE! THAT YOU, A BACKWARDS, JUNGLE-DWELLING SAVAGE ... AND A WOMAN NO LESS...>
<HEY!>
<BUT DON'T YOU KNOW THAT TREE BARK IS THE LEAST CONDUCTIVE SUBSTANCE KNOWN TO MAN? IT'S A MIRACLE THAT ABOMINATION WORKS AT ALL.>

<LOOK HERE ... WHY DON'T YOU LEAVE THIS MISERABLE ISLAND PARADISE BEHIND AND COME WITH ME? YOU CAN GET A PROPER EDUCATION, BUILD COMPUTERS WITH DECENT MATERIALS, PILOT MY AIRSHIP AND BE MY CHILD BRIDE.>
<SOUNDS GREAT!>
<EXCEPT FOR THAT LAST BIT.>

<NOW MIGHT BE THE TIME TO TELL YOUR RELATIVES THEY WON'T BE INVITED TO THE WEDDING.>

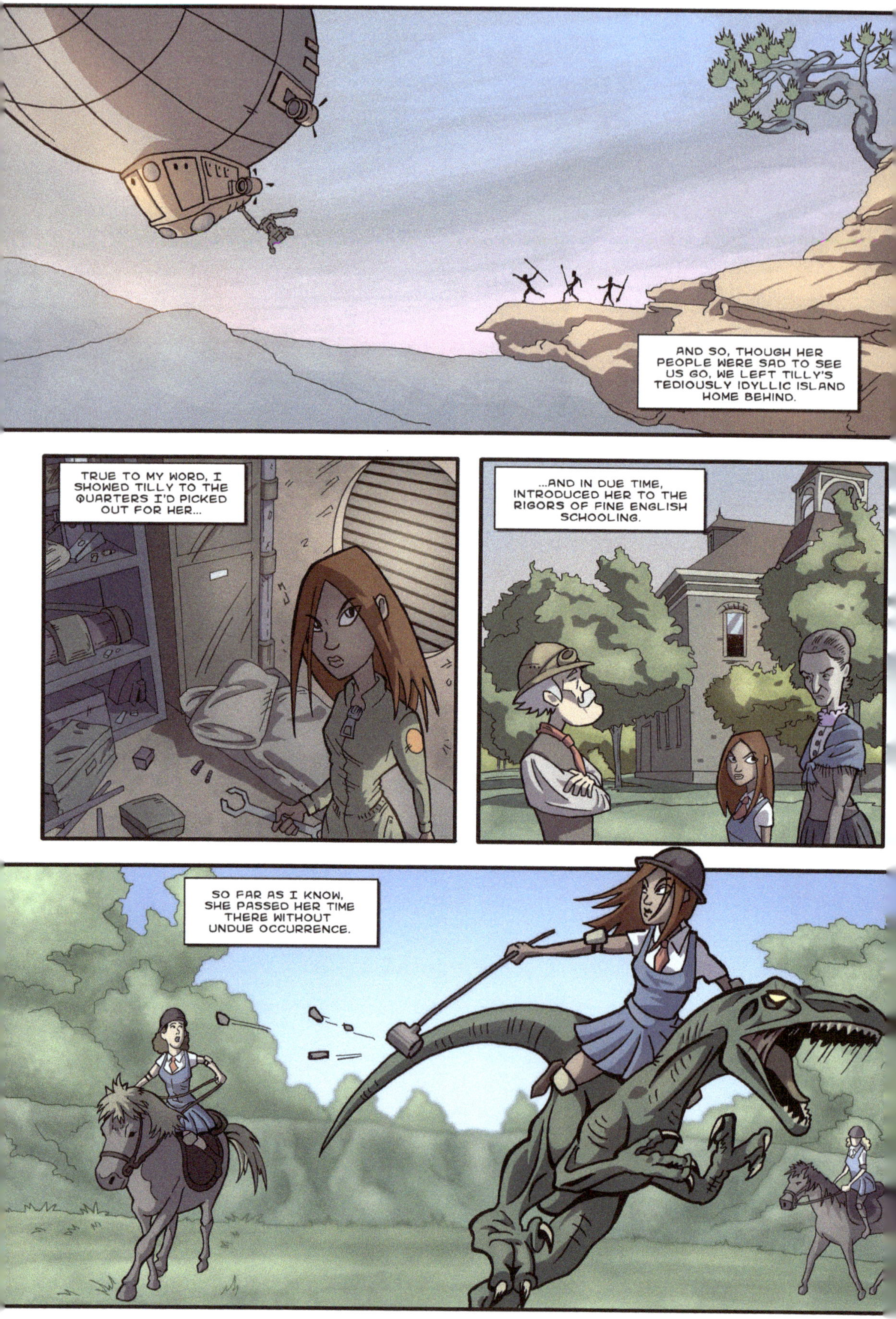

AND SO, THOUGH HER PEOPLE WERE SAD TO SEE US GO, WE LEFT TILLY'S TEDIOUSLY IDYLLIC ISLAND HOME BEHIND.

ANYWAY, THAT'S MORE THAN ENOUGH ABOUT TILLY.
WEREN'T YOU IN THE MIDDLE OF SOME KIND OF TRAGIC, FISH-RELATED LIFE STORY?
TRAGIC. YES.
AND FISH-RELATED TOO.
NO MORE COULD I STAND THE TRIALS OF POVERTY AND FAILURE.
NO MORE COULD I TOLERATE THE MOCKERY OF MY BRETHREN.
YET, WHAT CHOICE DID I HAVE?
ONLY ONE.
I COULD GO WHERE NO FISHERMAN DARED GO.

TO MONSTER ISLAND!

THE WATER
WAS CALM.
THE SKIES WERE
PERFECTLY BLUE.

I WAS NOT
AFRAID.
WHAT GREATER CRUELTIES COULD
FATE HOLD IN STORE THAN
THOSE I'D ALREADY ENDURED?

I CAST MY
NETS...

AND DREW FORTH A
HAUL THE LIKES
OF WHICH I'D
NEVER DREAMT.

BUT THE PRODIGIES OF
THAT DAY WERE ONLY
JUST BEGINNING.

YOU MAY IMAGINE HOW ASTONISHED I WAS AS WORDS BEGAN TO FORM UNSUMMONED IN MY MIND.
IT SOON BECAME APPARENT THAT THESE STRANGE DENIZENS OF THE SEA INTENDED ME NO HARM.
THEY TOLD ME OF HOW THEY HAD BEEN CAST OUT BY THEIR MONSTROUS KIN.
SPYING MY BOAT, THEY HAD COME TO ME IN HOPE OF FINDING PURPOSE TO THEIR MISERABLE LIVES.
HOW STRANGE, THAT WE POOR OUTCASTS SHOULD BE THROWN TOGETHER SO BY DESTINY!
YET, WAS IT SO STRANGE AT ALL? THE MORE TIME I SPENT IN THEIR COMPANY, THE MORE I UNDERSTOOD WHY FATE HAD THRUST US INTO EACH OTHER'S PATHS.
WE MUST FIGHT CRIME TOGETHER!

I CALL IT A MIDGARD SLING. IT'S MOSTLY RUM AND MILK

WITH JUST A DASH OF POWDERED SNAKE.

HMM. MOST UNEXPECTED.

MAY I ASK, THEN, WHILST WE ARE ON THE SUBJECT OF WHATEVER IT WAS WE WERE JUST TALKING ABOUT, HOW YOU CAME BY THIS FINE URSINE MANSERVANT?

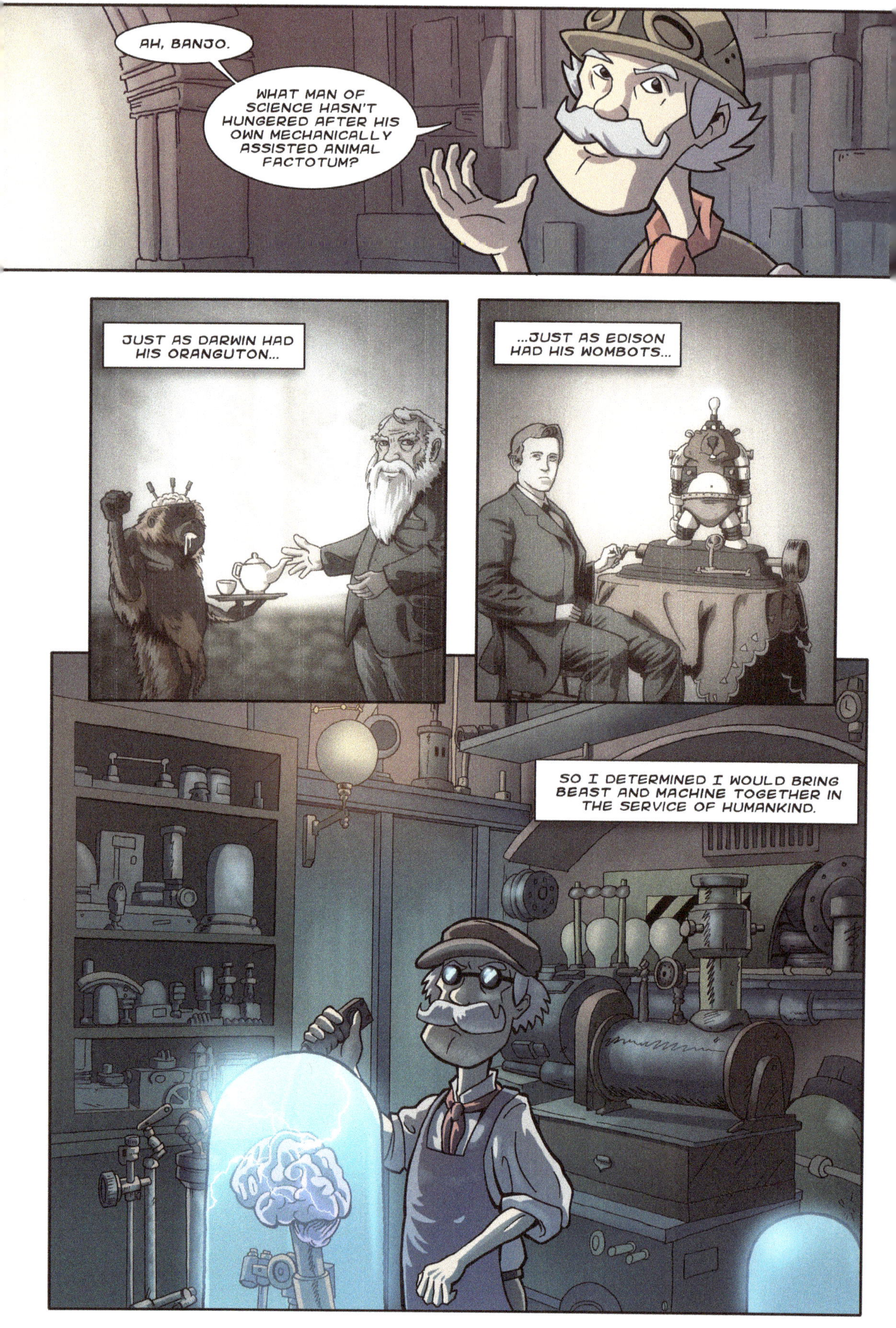

JUST AS DARWIN HAD HIS ORANGUTON...

...JUST AS EDISON HAD HIS WOMBOTS...

SO I DETERMINED I WOULD BRING BEAST AND MACHINE TOGETHER IN THE SERVICE OF HUMANKIND.

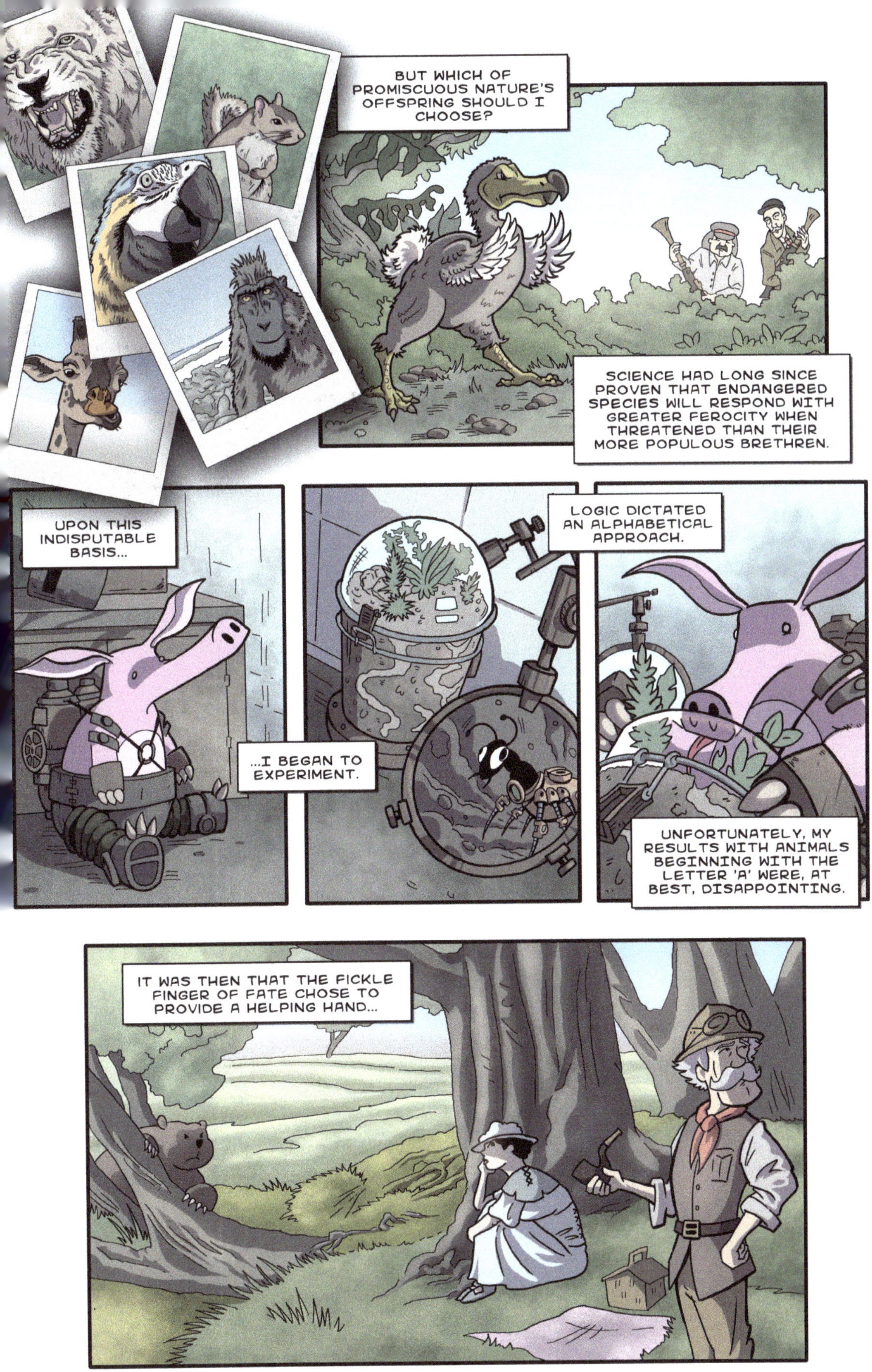

BUT WHICH OF PROMISCUOUS NATURE'S OFFSPRING SHOULD I CHOOSE?

SCIENCE HAD LONG SINCE PROVEN THAT ENDANGERED SPECIES WILL RESPOND WITH GREATER FEROCITY WHEN THREATENED THAN THEIR MORE POPULOUS BRETHREN.

UPON THIS INDISPUTABLE BASIS...

...I BEGAN TO EXPERIMENT.

LOGIC DICTATED AN ALPHABETICAL APPROACH.

UNFORTUNATELY, MY RESULTS WITH ANIMALS BEGINNING WITH THE LETTER 'A' WERE, AT BEST, DISAPPOINTING.

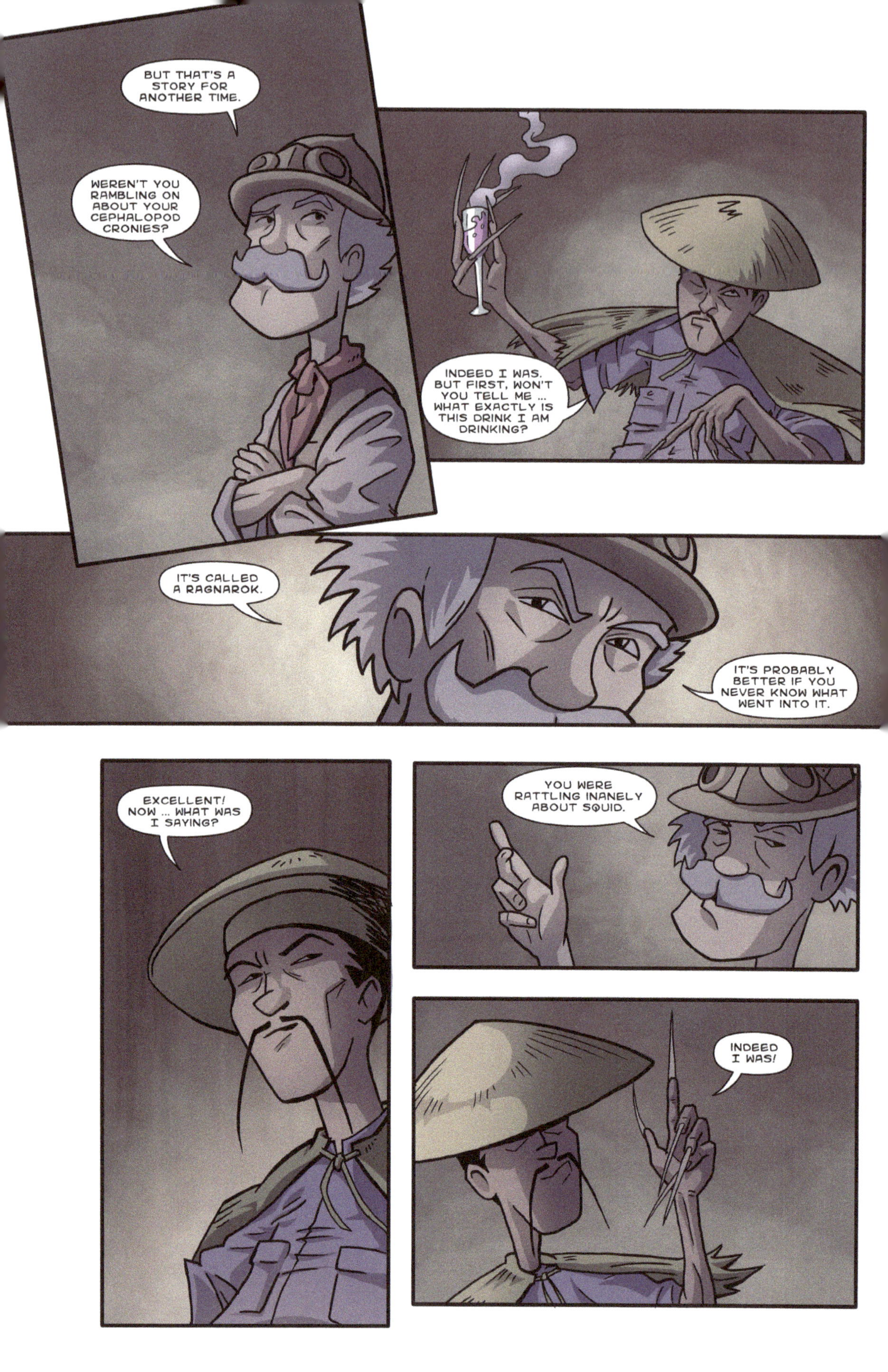

BUT THAT'S A STORY FOR ANOTHER TIME.

WEREN'T YOU RAMBLING ON ABOUT YOUR CEPHALOPOD CRONIES?

INDEED I WAS. BUT FIRST, WON'T YOU TELL ME ... WHAT EXACTLY IS THIS DRINK I AM DRINKING?

IT'S CALLED A RAGNAROK.

IT'S PROBABLY BETTER IF YOU NEVER KNOW WHAT WENT INTO IT.

MY FIRST DIFFICULTY WAS IN FINDING A KUNG FU MASTER WILLING TO TRAIN SQUID.

SUCH THINGS ARE HARDER THAN YOU MIGHT IMAGINE.

FINALLY, HIGH IN A MOUNTAINSIDE TEMPLE, I FOUND THE ONE MAN WHO COULD HELP ME.

THROUGH MANY A LONG MONTH, WE TOILED TO HONE OUR SKILLS...

UNTIL WAS BORN THE ULTIMATE IN CEPHALOPODIC JUSTICE ...

SQUID SQUAD 7!

AHEM. NOT TO SEEM CONTRARY, BUT AREN'T THERE ONLY THREE OF THEM THERE?
SO WE COME TO THE MOMENT OF MY GREATEST SHAME.
FOOL WAS I TO CONFRONT THE INFAMOUSLY CALAMARI-LOVING PIRATES OF MARINARA BAY!

FORGIVE ME ... MY GRIEF FORBIDS ME TO SAY MORE.

PROFESSOR, TO RELIEVE MY ANGUISHED SOUL, PERHAPS YOU COULD TELL ME OF THE ONE YOU CALL 'WIFFLES'?

WELL ... WIFFLES IS MY BUTLER.

AND A NINJA...

WHO'S JUST TEMPORARILY PARALYSED YOU FROM THE ADAM'S APPLE DOWNWARDS.

WHAT IS THIS TREACHERY? TO MY AID, MY FLACCID BRETHREN!
NOT TO INTERFERE, BUT ISN'T YOUR COMMUNICATION WITH THOSE REVOLTING SPECIMENS BASED ON SOME SORT OF TELEPATHY?
I DOUBT THAT WILL WORK SO WELL WHEN YOU'VE ENOUGH ALCOHOL IN YOU TO PICKLE A GOAT.
OF COURSE, I MIGHT BE WRONG.

OR NOT.

THWUNK

ARISTOTLE ON VOODOO
THUMP!

IT'S TRUE WHAT THEY SAY ABOUT YOU, PROFESSOR ...
YOU ARE A FIEND IN HUMAN FORM!
WHAT DID HE SAY?
SOUNDED TO ME LIKE, "THANK YOU FOR THE COCKIAILS!"
WELL. QUITE RIGHT.

SO WHERE TO NOW, PROFESSOR?

DIDN'T YOU HEAR THE MAN? WHY, TO MONSTER ISLAND, OF COURSE!

ER ... WHICH ONE?
WHICH ONE INDEED? FIND OUT ... IN THE NEXT ISSUE OF ENDANGERED WEAPON B!

Sketchbook 1: The Professor

Designing a character can be a very complex process, with lots of important factors to consider. You need to be able to take one look at him and 'get' the character, understand his motivations, his demeanour, believe in him as a real person and most important of all is 'how big can you make his moustache?'

Bob.

ENDANGERED WEAPON B

AND THE MONSTERS OF MONSTER ISLAND

SO WHERE TO NOW, PROFESSOR?

WHY, TO MONSTER ISLAND, OF COURSE!

ER ... WHICH ONE?

TWO MONSTER ISLANDS? WHAT MYSTERY IS THIS?
THEN AGAIN, PERHAPS IT'S NOT **ENTIRELY** SURPRISING. MONSTERS HAVE NEVER BEEN KNOWN TO GET ALONG WITH EACH OTHER.

LET'S TRY THIS ONE, THEN.

IT'S NOT AS IF I DON'T HAVE SOME READING TO CATCH UP ON.

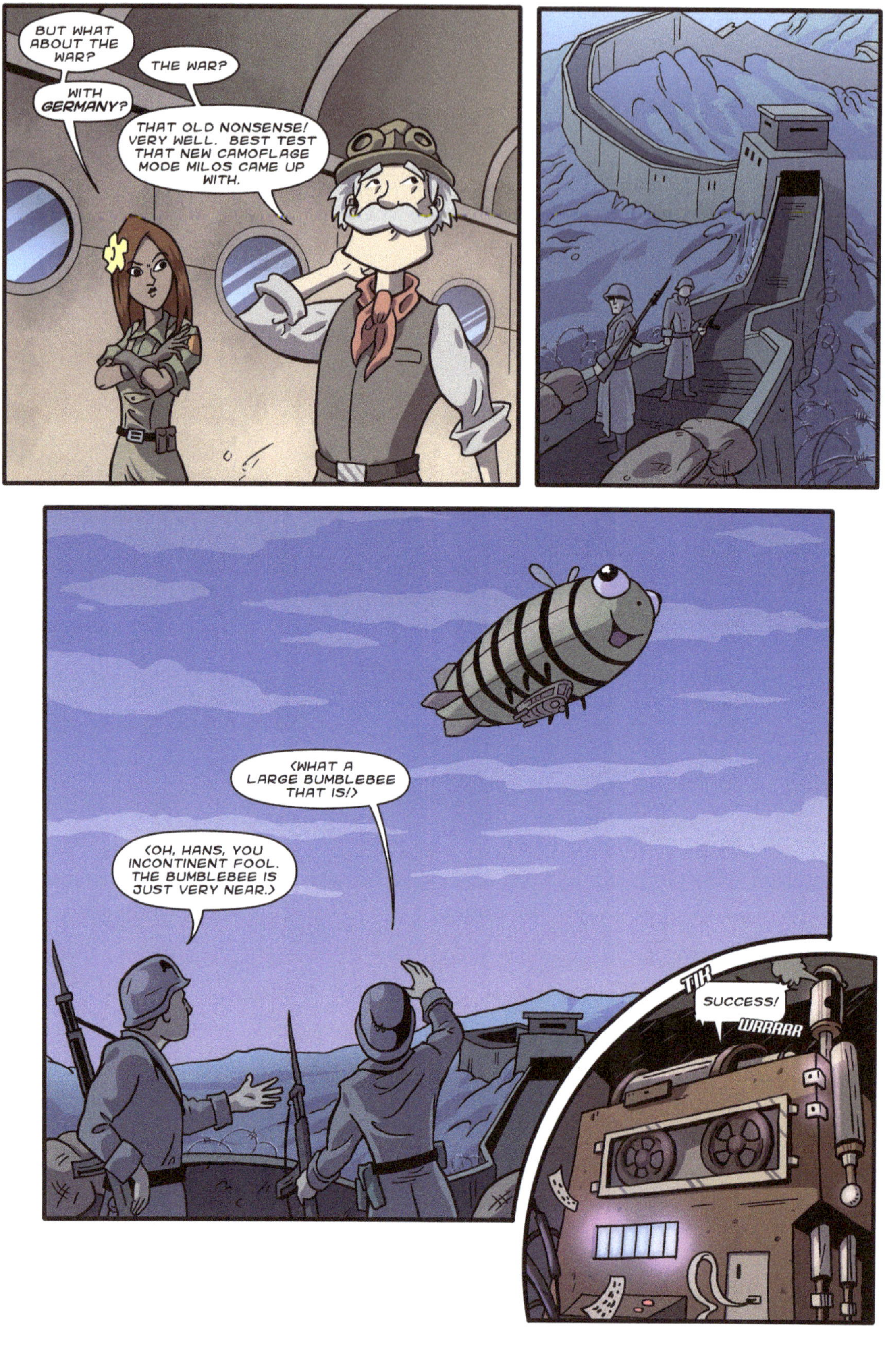

<WHAT A LARGE BUMBLEBEE THAT IS!>

<OH, HANS, YOU INCONTINENT FOOL. THE BUMBLEBEE IS JUST VERY NEAR.>

TIK

SUCCESS!

WRRRRR

CREEPY.
THE WORD, MY DEAR, IS **TEUTONIC**.

NOPE. **DEFINITELY** CREEPY.
I'M SURE THERE'S ABSOLUTELY NOTHING WHATSOEVER TO BE ALARMED BY.

WHEEZE
HUFFF
WHEEZE
HUFFF
WHEEZE
THRUNK

VELCOME ... TO THE HOME OF DRACULA!

DRACULA. IS THAT A GERMAN NAME?
NO. NOT VEALLY.
ARE YOU QUITE SURE?
VOSITIVE. NOW VON'T YOU JOIN ME FOR ... DINNER?

SO THIS IS YOUR CASTLE THEN, IS IT?
ABSOLUTELY. ZIS DEFINITELY IS MY CASTLE.

SPLENDID! MIND IF WE HAVE A LOOK AROUND?
YES, I MIND! YOU VUST STAY FOR ... DINNER.
I'M AFRAID WIFFLES MADE HAM SANDWICHES BEFORE WE SET OUT. COULDN'T EAT ANOTHER THING!
BUT DON'T LET US KEEP YOU...
NO! VAIT!

CHOMP

THWACK!

BANJO? WHAT ARE YOU DOING? THIS IS NO TIME FOR LOLLYGAGGING!
THWACK!
THWACK!
THWACK!
THWACK!

AHA! NOW THIS IS MORE LIKE IT.

HMM. FUNNY HOW ONE'S EYE IS DRAWN TO THAT PARTICULAR VOLUME.

So strange an accident has happened to us that I cannot forbear recording it, although it is very probable that you will see me before these papers can come into your possession.

THE CONTINUING ADVENTURES OF VICTOR VON FRANKENSTEIN.
A JOURNAL.
Oh, tragic fate! That the world should consider Victor Frankenstein dead. And all because of that fat liar Captain Walton!
Let posterity know that the rumours of my death have been greatly exagerated.

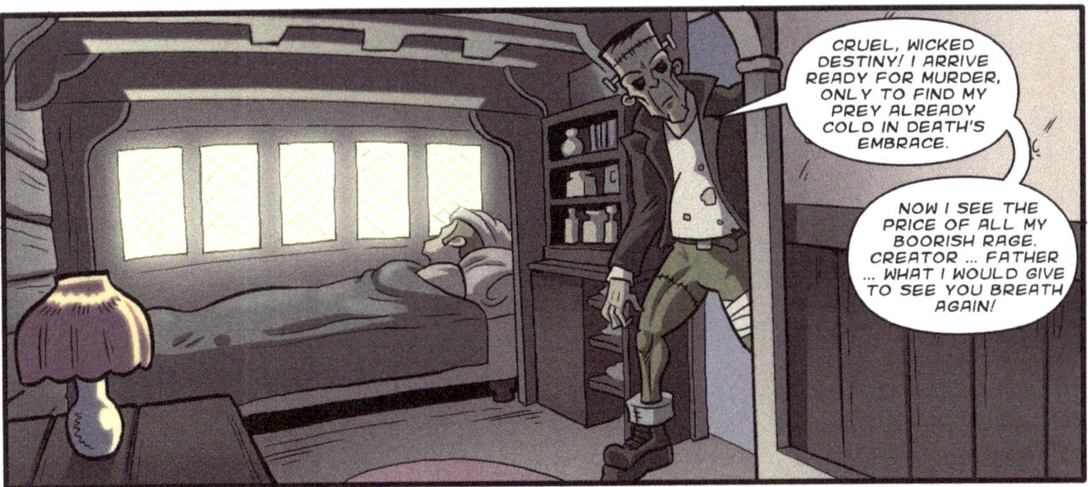
CRUEL, WICKED DESTINY! I ARRIVE READY FOR MURDER, ONLY TO FIND MY PREY ALREADY COLD IN DEATH'S EMBRACE.
NOW I SEE THE PRICE OF ALL MY BOORISH RAGE. CREATOR ... FATHER ... WHAT I WOULD GIVE TO SEE YOU BREATH AGAIN!

WHO'S THAT? CAN'T YOU SEE I'M TRYING TO SLEEP?

AAAAAAGH!

YOU LIVE! AS THOUGH IN ANSWER TO THIS MONSTER'S FOOLISH PRAYER, YOU LIVE!
ER ... APPARENTLY.
MASTER, CAN YOU EVER FORGIVE YOUR IGNORANT CREATION?
YOU KILLED MY BROTHER! AND MY BELOVED ELIZABETH!
BUT ALL RIGHT
SPITEFUL CHANCE, IF IT BE YOUR WILL, LET FRANKENSTEIN RECONCILE WITH HIS WAYWARD CREATION...
AND LET THEM TEAM UP TO BEAT UP OTHER MONSTERS!
THIS FRANKENSTEIN SOUNDS LIKE A MAN AFTER MY OWN HEART.

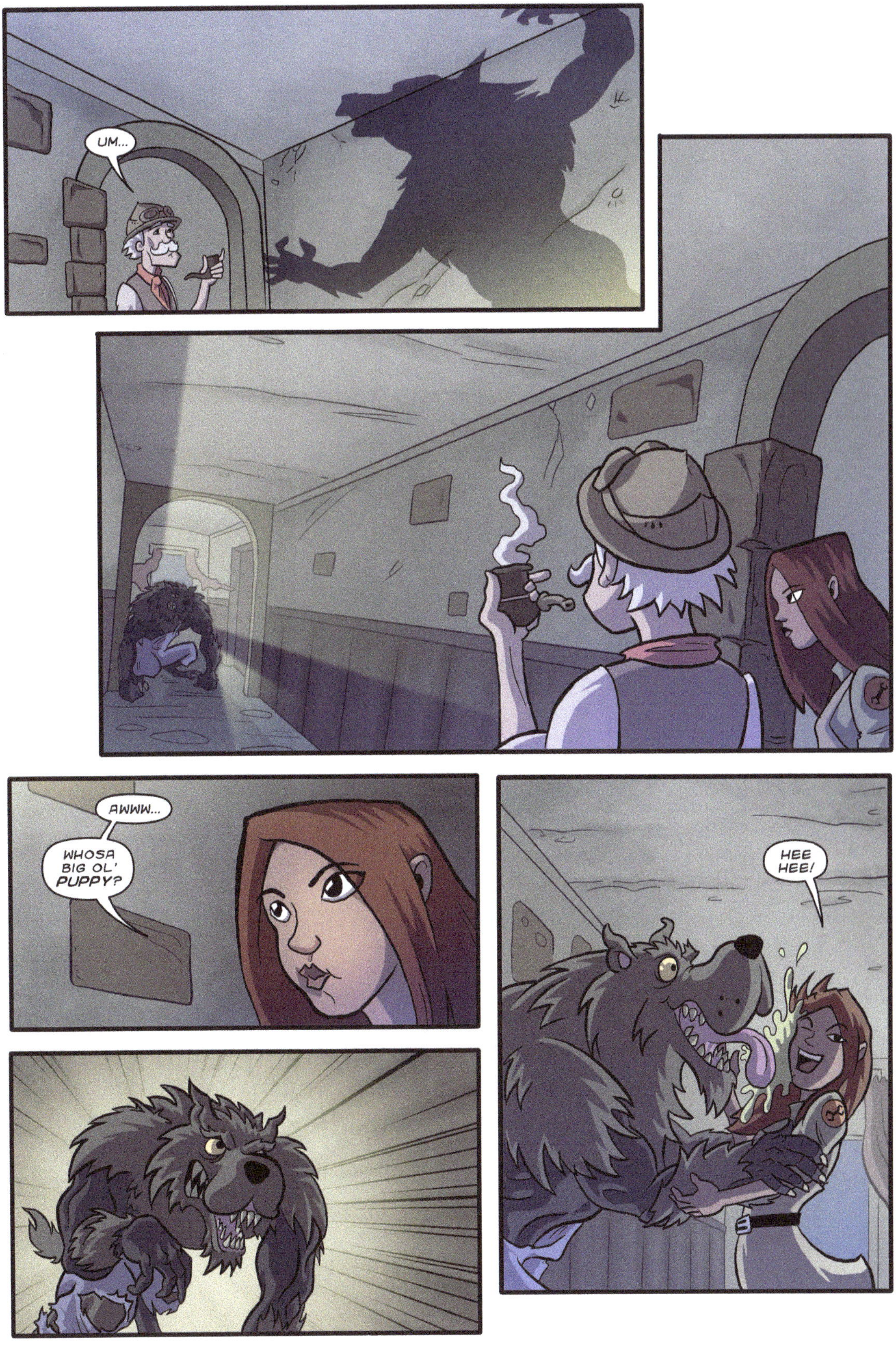

UM...

WHO WANTS A HUG? WHICH PUPPY WANTS A SPECIAL PUPPY HUG?
BANJO, PLEASE DO SOMETHING ABOUT THAT PESTERSOME BEAST.

SQUEEE-
KRITCH!

SQUEE-EE-EEEEEEE!

AAAWW WOOOOOO OOOOO...
AW.
NOW THAT THAT NONSENSE IS DONE WITH, WHY DON'T YOU GET ON WITH READING ABOUT THIS FRANKENSTEIN CHAP?
HUMMPH.
STOOPID FRANKENSTEIN.
"ANYWAY. ALL IT IS IS PAGES AND PAGES OF THEM BEATING UP ON MONSTERS."

MONSTERS, YOU SAY?
THIS IS STARTING TO MAKE A CURIOUS SORT OF SENSE.
THE MUMMY
DRACULA
THE PHANTOM
METALUNA MUTANT
WOLF MAN
CREATURE FROM THE LAGOON
MOLE MEN

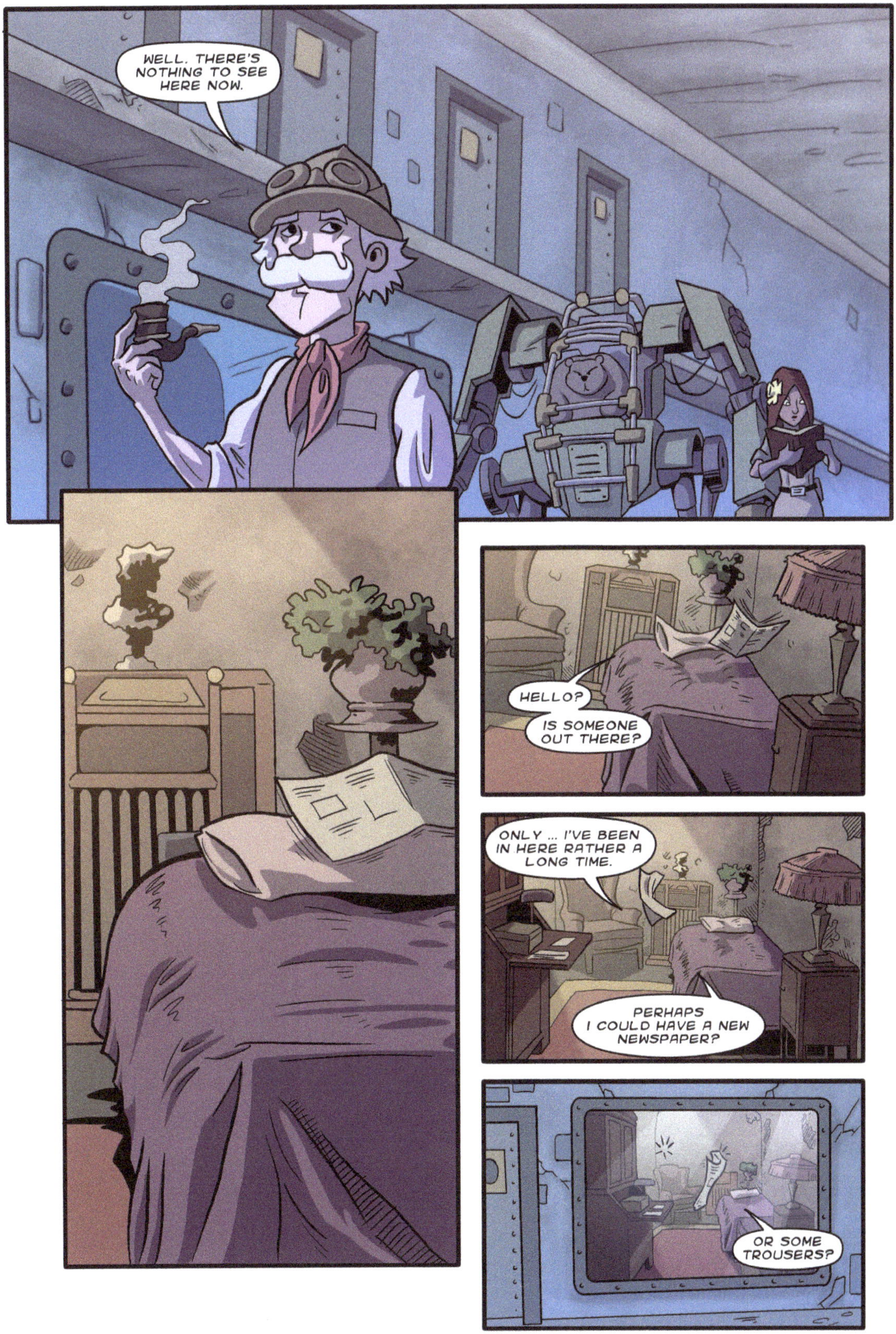

WELL. THERE'S NOTHING TO SEE HERE NOW.

HELLO?

IS SOMEONE OUT THERE?

GAAAAAH!

THUD!

OOF!

CRUNK!

TIRED ...
SO **VERY**
TIRED.

YOU WOULDN'T BE THE SEVERED HEAD OF **DOCTOR FRANKENSTEIN'S MONSTER**, BY ANY CHANCE?
I AM IT.

IF YOU DON'T MIND A PERSONAL COMMENT FROM A STRANGER, I'D SAY YOU LOOK A LITTLE THE WORSE FOR WEAR.
I HAVE PULLED MYSELF UP FROM THE DEPTHS, ALL **SEVEN HUNDRED AND FORTY SIX** STAIRS ... USING ONLY MY TEETH AND EYEBROWS.

REMARKABLE! FROM THOSE DEPTHS, YOU SAY? FUNNILY ENOUGH, THAT HAPPENS TO BE JUST WHERE WE'RE HEADING.
BRING HIM ALONG, BANJO. AND READ ON, TILLY GIRL.

NOT AGAIN! **NOT AGAIN!**

JULY 8TH
19--
BORED. SO VERY BORED.

PERHAPS A GAME OF CHESS, MASTER?

PAH!

JULY 15TH
19--
CAN IT REALLY BE THAT THERE ARE NO MONSTERS LEFT TO DEFEAT?

JULY 18TH
19--
THEN ... THANKS ENTIRELY TO MY *CRUSHING BOREDOM*, A BREAKTHROUGH!

CREATURE! PACK MY *GUNS!*

AS WE BATTLED OUR WAY THROUGH THE MONSTERS OF THE *OTHER* MONSTER ISLAND, A PLAN BEGAN TO FORM IN MY FEBRILE BRAIN...
A GRAND PLAN! A PLAN SUCH AS NO OTHER SANE MAN COULD EVER HAVE CONCEIVED!
BWA HA HA! HA HA! BWA HA HA HA!
AND IT JUST GOES ON LIKE THAT FOR THE NEXT SEVEN PAGES.

I'D ALWAYS KNOWN THAT MY MASTER WAS A FEW PEBBLES SHORT OF A ZEN GARDEN. BUT THIS ... THIS ... WAS TOO MUCH!
SPEED READING, PLEASE, TILLY! I THINK WE MAY HAVE WANDERED INTO A SPOT OF BOTHER.

I HAD A **GREAT BIG PILE** OF GIANT MONSTER PARTS.

AND A PREDISPOSITION FOR **MAKING THINGS** OUT OF BITS OF **OTHER THINGS**.

AND A DISPROPORTIONATELY **HUGE BRAIN** THAT WAS **FAR** TOO SPECIAL FOR MY MISERABLE HUMAN FRAME.

IT WAS OBVIOUS WHAT I HAD TO DO!

FOOOM
RAAAAAK
GRRRR
THOMP
THOMP
THOMP

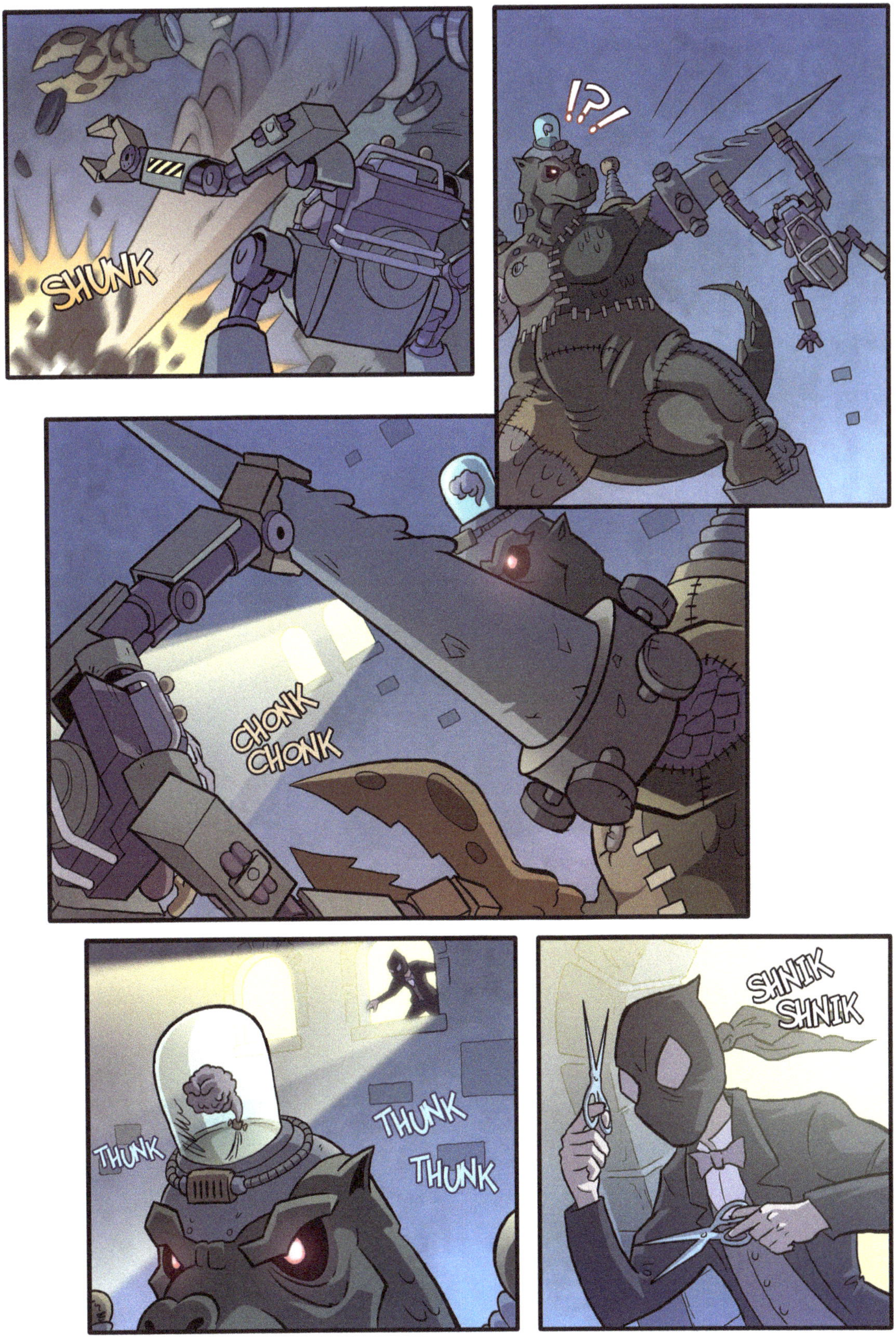

SHUNK
!?!
CHONK
CHONK

SHNIK
SHNIK
SHNIK
SHNIK
RAAAAAK

CRRRZZZ ... WHO **DARES** DEFILE THE CAREFULLY HAND-SEWED **MAJESTY** OF MEGAFRANKENSTEIN?

CREATURE? IS THAT **YOU?** THIS IS VERY DISAPPOINTING.

I'M SORRY MASTER. BUT YOU'RE INSANE, AND YOU DESTROYED MY BODY.

YOUR POINT?

DR FRANKENSTEIN? I'M **THE PROFESSOR**, AND THESE ARE MY TRAVELLING COMPANIONS. WE'RE ALL GREAT FANS OF YOUR WORK.
I'M NOT.
EXCELLENT! BANJO, BRING HIM ALONG, WON'T YOU?

SO, DOCTOR.

LET'S TALK ABOUT REANIMATING THE DEAD.

Spot the Similarities

AS EVERY FAN OF SCIENCE KNOWS, CHARLES DARWIN AND THOMAS EDISON WERE THE GREATEST OF ADVERSARIES, THEIR FIERCE MUTUAL JEALOUSY AND ARGUMENTS OVER WHO INVENTED THE TRACTION-POWERED LOOM THE CAUSE OF MANY AN EPISTOLARY SPAT AND DRIVE-BY WATER BALLOONING. BUT FOR ALL THEIR DIFFERENCES, THEY DID HAVE A FEW THINGS IN COMMON. CAN YOU SPOT FIVE OF THEM?

MISFORTUNE HAS STRUCK!

WHILST OUT ADVENTURING, THE PROFESSOR WAS SET UPON BY PARTICULARLY VORACIOUS MOTHS, AND NOW HIS FAVOURITE CLOTHES ARE ALL IN TATTERS. AS IF THAT WEREN'T DISASTER ENOUGH, HE'S DUE TO MEET THE EMPRESS OF ZANZIBAR FOR AFTERNOON TEA. WHAT OUTFIT CAN HE POSSIBLY COBBLE TOGETHER THAT WILL IMPRESS HER AUGUST HIGHNESS, WHILST PROTECTING HIM FROM THE ISLAND'S NOTORIOUS, FIRE-BREATHING SLOTHS ...THE DEADLIEST AND SLOWEST PREDATOR IN ALL THE WORLD? WHO CAN POSSIBILITY EXTRICATE HIM FROM SOCIAL EMBARRASSMENT AND FIRST-DEGREE TOASTING? ONLY YOU, DEAR READER ... ONLY YOU!

Sketchbook 2: Tilly

Tilly was the character who changed the most between finishing the pilot episode and starting on the graphic novel. I went through several different designs before arriving at this point. She had to look practical, capable, and most of all angry.

Bob.

ENDANGERED WEAPON B

ENDTRODUCTION

The story you're about to read is the first Endangered Weapon story I wrote, and the first Bob drew. So shouldn't it be at the beginning? Well, yes and no. But mainly no. You see, before Endangered Weapon B was Endangered Weapon B, it was a vague concept for a Manga pastiche about crime fighting pandas in mechanical suits - the joke being, pandas are hugely lazy and ill-suited to fighting crime. Most of that idea got dropped when I decided to write a strip for a British anthology comic running at the time and wanted a story that could be told in a few pages. So multiple pandas became one - named Pongo - and I started wondering why a panda might be running around in a mechanised suit if he wasn't fighting crime.

Somehow, that led to the Professor, and to Tilly and Wiffles and Milos - and from there, inevitably, to Nazi space-dolphins. I wrote my story and it was accepted, but the editor requested that I change the panda to some other animal, because a rival company was putting out a lot of books involving pandas just then. Some strange ideas were kicked about before Pongo became Banjo; this came dangerously close to being a series about a mechanised kangaroo. But I revised my script and all was well - until the editor wrote to say his comic was closing down.

It was soon after that and a certain amount of cursing that I stumbled across Bob Molesworth. I didn't even know Bob was an artist; he was involved with a little indie comic empire back then, and I assumed he was a publisher. I ran my script by him and he said he liked it. A few months later, when I wrote asking if he was still interested, Bob sent me back the pages that follow: the first ever Endangered Weapon story, drawn, lettered and coloured.

Seeing these characters through the delirious cartoon lens of Bob's art, I knew I couldn't just leave it there. Thus was born the book you hold in your hands. It's been a long, hard journey since then, but also the most fun I've had writing anything ever. Imagine having a superpower where you can write something like "fire breathing sloth" and a few hours later a picture of a fire breathing sloth appears in your inbox. How awesome would that be?

Here, then, is the first issue - but not really the first issue - of Endangered Weapon B. Onwards, by Odin!

David Tallerman

THE PROFESSOR: EXPLORER, INVENTOR, ECCENTRIC.
ABOVE ... ABOARD THE AIRSHIP VALHALLA.
LOOKS LIKE THOSE DAMNED SAVAGES AIN'T SO HAPPY ABOUT YOU STEALING THEIR SACRED KWANGA BIRD, PROFESSOR.
TILLY TOBEGA: AIRSHIP PILOT, TECHNICIAN.
CAN'T BE HELPED! IF MY THEORIES ARE CORRECT, THIS BIRD'S BLOOD CONTAINS THE CURE TO ANY NUMBER OF UNFORTUNATE SOCIAL SICKNESSES.
AND REMEMBER ... IF I HADN'T RESCUED YOU FROM YOUR IDYLLIC LIFE OF DRUDGERY, YOU'D STILL BE ONE OF THOSE 'SAVAGES'.
DON'T REMIND ME.
BUT I STILL AIN'T GONNA MARRY YOU, DIRTY OLD MAN!
KEEP GOING, PROF, MILOS SHOULD BE READY WITH AN ESCAPE PLAN.
MILOS: SUPERCOMPUTER
TIK ... TIK ... TIK ... BEAR!
YOU ALWAYS SAY THAT.

BANJO: MECHANISED COMBAT GRIZZLY

ENDANGERED WEAPON B

GRAWRAWRAWR

STORY BY DAVID TALLERMAN
ART BY BOB MOLESWORTH

LATER. THE VALHALLA. TEA TIME.
MORE KWANGA TEA, PLEASE, WIFFLES.
DRING! DRING!

WIFFLES: NINJA BUTLER.
"IT'S GENERAL WINCEFOSTER-SMYTHE HERE, FROM THE HOME OFFICE."

"WE NEED YOUR HELP, PROFESSOR. IT'S THOSE DRATTED NAZIS! THEY'RE UP TO SOME KIND OF SHENNANIGANS IN THE PACIFIC. YOU MUST REMEMBER EVIL ISLAND, PROFESSOR, WHERE DOCTOR DOGMADOG STOLE YOUR..."

YES, YES. I'VE TOLD YOU BEFORE, GENERAL: THOSE NAZI RAPSCALLIONS DON'T BOTHER ME, AND I DON'T BOTHER THEM.
"WE'RE PREPARED TO MAKE YOU A ONE-TIME OFFER ... AN AFTERNOON'S UNINTERUPTED ACCESS TO THE TOP-SECRET WING OF THE BRITISH LIBRARY."

THE MAMMOTH BOOK OF ZOMBIFICATION
DONE!

LATER...
EVIL ISLAND.
IT DOESN'T APPEAR TO HAVE GOT ANY LESS EVIL SINCE I WAS LAST HERE.
WELL, AT LEAST THEY'VE SPRUCED THE PLACE UP A BIT.
THOR'S TESTICLES! LOOKS LIKE THEY'VE SPOTTED US. TO THE GUNS, WIFFLES!
BRAP
BRAP
BRAP

THOSE PILOTS ARE A LITTLE ODD LOOKING, EVEN BY THIRD REICH STANDARDS.

HMM?

SHSHSHOOOOOOM

NOW THERE'S SOMETHING YOU DON'T SEE EVERY DAY.

TIME TO TEST THOSE MODIFICATIONS WE MADE, TILLY OLD GIRL.

YET LATER...

THE MOON.

BY ODIN ...
SPACE DOLPHINS!

YES! SPACE DOLPHINS!

WHAT ON EARTH ARE YOU DOING ON THE MOON?
YOUR SO-CALLED MOON SHALL BE THE CAPITAL OF OUR GALACTIC EMPIRE.
THAT SEEMS FAIR. BUT WHAT ABOUT THE NAZIS? WHY HAVE YOU BEEN TRAFFICKING WITH THOSE GOOSE-STEPPING BANDITS?

BY SUPPLYING OUR HUMAN ALLIES WITH SUPERIOR WEAPONS AND DAPPER UNIFORMS WE WILL PLUNGE YOUR CIVILISATION INTO CHAOS!
THEN, WHEN YOUR WORLD LIES IN RUINS, WE WILL CRUSH YOU ALL BENEATH OUR MOIST RUBBERY FLIPPERS.
WE GET SO BORED UP HERE.
BANJO, I THINK IT'S TIME WE SHOWED THESE PROFITEERING BLOWHOLE BREATHERS WHAT'S FOR.
BANJO?

BUT... HOW DID YOU KNOW THAT URSUS ARCTOS HORRIBILIS HAS A WEAKNESS FOR FOOD?
WE LIVE ON THE MOON AND YOU SHAVED APES HAVE BARELY INVENTED TELEVISION. WE READ A LOT OF BOOKS.
NOW PREPARE FOR YOUR ICKY DOOM!
BANJO!
BANJO!
URP.

BANJO, GET HERE RIGHT NOW OR THERE'LL BE NO MORE VISITS TO MISSY AT YELLOWSTONE PARK!

ROAAAGH!!!

EEP
EEP
WHOOOP
DANGER!
DO NOT PULL,
EVER.

GROAWWWW!!!

I KNEW SOMETHING FISHY WAS GOING ON, PROFESSOR!
DOLPHINS ARE MAMMALS, YOU SILLY GIRL.
AINT NEVER GONNA MARRY YOU...
FIN!

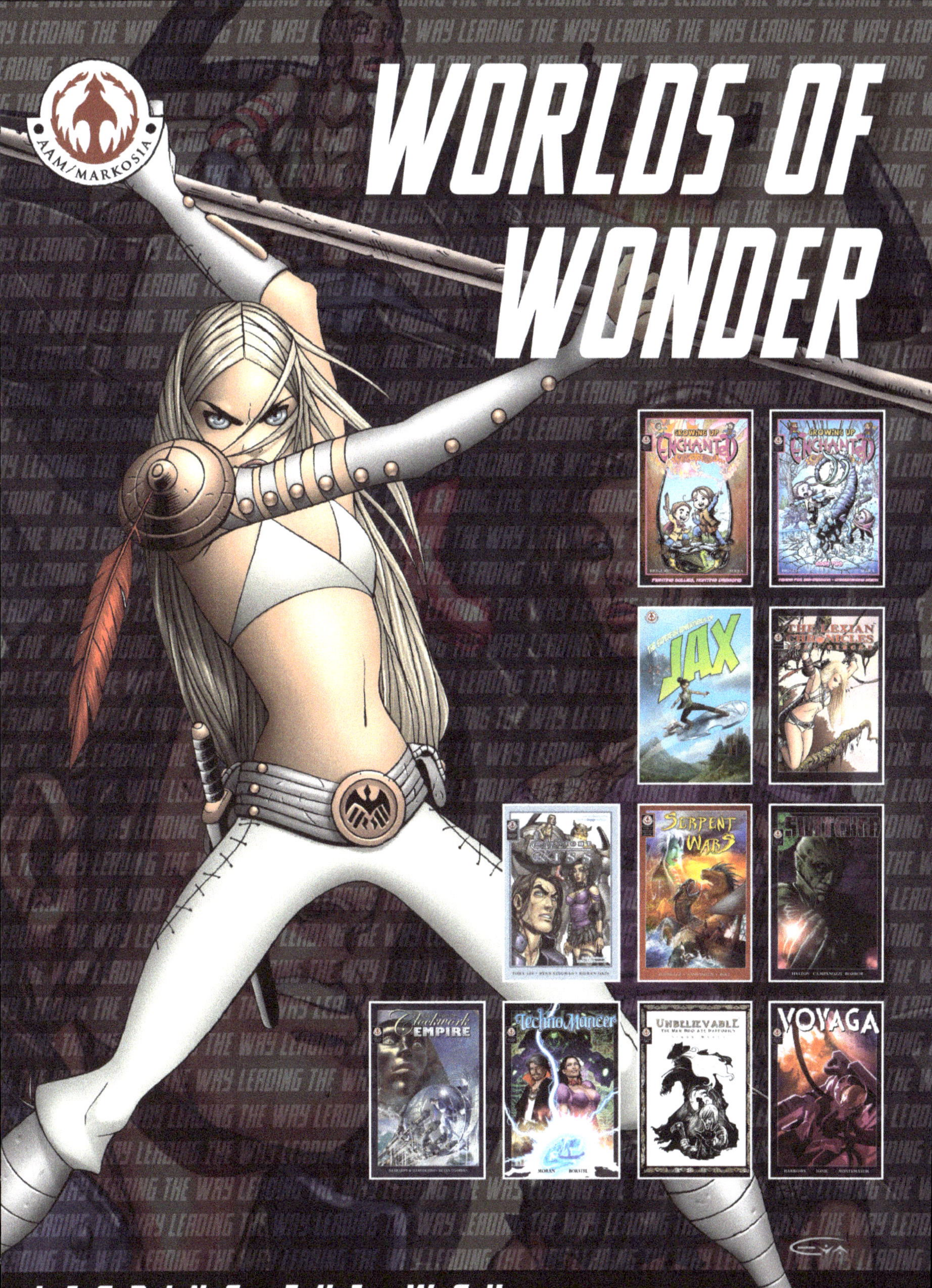
WWW.MARKOSIA.COM
AAM/MARKOSIA
WORLDS OF WONDER
GROWING UP ENCHANTED
GROWING UP ENCHANTED
JAX
THE LEXIAN CHRONICLES
SERPENT WARS
CLOCKWORK EMPIRE
TECHNOMANCER
UNBELIEVABLE
VOYAGA
LEADING THE WAY

www.ingramcontent.com/pod-product-compliance
Ingram Content Group UK Ltd.
Pitfield, Milton Keynes, MK11 3LW, UK
UKHW061953290726
14090UKWH00021B/1201